GO **Nick JR** DIEGO GO!™

Diego and Papi to the Rescue

by Wendy Wax
illustrated by John Hom

Simon Spotlight/Nick Jr.
New York London Toronto Sydney

Based on the TV series *Go, Diego, Go!*™ as seen on Nick Jr.®

SIMON SPOTLIGHT
An imprint of Simon & Schuster Children's Publishing Division
1230 Avenue of the Americas, New York, New York 10020
© 2007 Viacom International Inc. All rights reserved.
NICK JR., *Go, Diego, Go!*, and all related titles, logos,
and characters are trademarks of Viacom International Inc.
Manufactured in the United States of America
First Edition
2 4 6 8 10 9 7 5 3 1
ISBN-13: 978-1-4169-2781-5
ISBN-10: 1-4169-2781-6

¡Hola! I'm Diego, and I'm an Animal Rescuer. This is my sister Alicia, and this is our *papi. Papi* is an Animal Expert too!

Do you hear something? It sounds like an animal is calling for help. Let's find out which animal it is.

Click the Camera will help us find the animal in trouble. Zoom through the forest to find the animal calling for help, Click!

Oh, no! There are two animals in trouble—two baby pygmy marmosets! They're in that tree near the waterfall! They look lost!

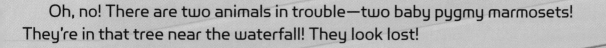

I know! My *papi* and I can help the baby pygmy marmosets find their *papi*! *Papi* says Alicia and I should check the computer to find out more about pygmy marmosets. That way we can figure out where *Papi* Pygmy Marmoset might be.

The computer says pygmy marmosets are the smallest monkeys in the world. Each pygmy marmoset weighs less than a grapefruit!

The computer also says that pygmy marmosets live high in trees and eat tree sap. Their coats help them blend in with the forest so they can hide.

Papi says that because pygmy marmosets eat tree sap, we can probably find *Papi* Pygmy Marmoset near the sap tree. Let's go rescue the babies and bring them to the sap tree to find their *papi*!

Here we go! Animal Rescuers away!
¡Al rescate! To the rescue!

I hear a waterfall! There it is! The baby pygmy marmosets must be up in this tree next to the waterfall. We just have to find a way to get to the top.

We can climb! Climb with us! Climb, climb! *¡Sube, sube!*

I hear a whistling noise. Who could be whistling?

Papi says pygmy marmosets make a whistling sound. So we're probably hearing the baby pygmy marmosets!

It *is* the baby pygmy marmosets! They say they were playing follow-the-leader in the tree branches while their *papi* was getting food for them, and now they're lost. Aw, we'll help you find your *papi*, babies!

Papi says that if *Papi* Pygmy Marmoset was getting food, then he must be at the sap tree. Let's go find him!

Papi knows a shortcut to the sap tree. We just have to find a way over the waterfall.

Rescue Pack can help! To help Rescue Pack transform into something that can get us over the waterfall, say *"¡Actívate!"*

Rescue Pack turned into a hot-air balloon! Great work, Rescue Pack! Now we can fly over the waterfall to get to the sap tree and *Papi* Pygmy Marmoset.

¡Excelente! We made it to the other side of the waterfall! And there's the sap tree! But wait! Why is the sap tree shaking?

It's the Bobo Brothers! They are dancing around the sap tree and making it shake. If we don't stop them, *Papi* Pygmy Marmoset could fall out of the tree.

Help me stop the Bobo Brothers! Shout "Freeze, Bobos!"

The Bobo Brothers said they are sorry. Thanks for helping me stop them. Now the sap tree isn't shaking anymore!

But why are the baby pygmy marmosets shaking now? Something is scaring them! Oh, no! A harpy eagle is flying toward us. Pygmy marmosets are afraid of harpy eagles. Let's help them hide so the harpy eagle will fly right past us.

Papi says their color helps them hide in the tree branches. Let's crouch down in the branches and hide like pygmy marmosets!

That was good hiding. The harpy eagle flew right past us!

But now I don't see *Papi* Pygmy Marmoset. Maybe he hid in the sap tree because he was scared by the harpy eagle too!

Papi says that *Papi* Pygmy Marmoset is probably using his dark coat to blend in with the tree.

Let's use the Spotting Scope to see if we can find him!

There's *Papi* Pygmy Marmoset! Let's tell him it's safe to come out of hiding now. Let's help the baby pygmy marmosets call to their *papi*. Call out *"¡Papi!"*

¡Hola, Papi Pygmy Marmoset! I'm Diego, and this is my *papi*. We brought your babies back to you!

Papi knows how much *Papi* Pygmy Marmoset must have missed his babies because he's a *papi* too!

Papi Pygmy Marmoset is so happy to have his babies back. Thank you for helping us bring them back to their *papi*. *¡Gracias!*

Now the pygmy marmosets can get some tree sap and have dinner together. First they need to make a hole in the tree. Then they suck out the yummy sap.

Papi says it's our dinnertime too. Let's go home!

Rescue complete!

¡Misión cumplida!

Did you know?

Teeny-weeny!

The pygmy marmoset is the smallest monkey in the world, weighing only a half a pound.

Busy days!

Pygmy marmosets are very active. They run, jump, and leap in trees and shrubs all day long.

Up in the trees!

The pygmy marmosets have dark bodies that help them stay camouflaged in the trees.

All in the family!

Pygmy marmosets live in family groups of two to six. Twins are born every five to six months.